Love to Draw...

Pokémon Go

Learn how to draw your favorite Pokémon Go characters!

Lucy Fairclough

ISBN: 1537620029

ISBN-13: 978-1537620022

Love to Draw... Pokémon Go

Drawing the characters from Pokémon is not only fun but a lot easier than you might think! With the help of this book, you'll discover how to draw them in no time at all. Here are a few tips to keep in mind whilst you're at it!

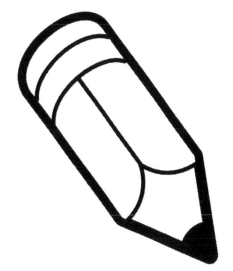

At the top of each image is some information about each character and also a star rating, the more gold stars the harder it is to draw! Maybe start off with a few one or two stars before working onto the more difficult ones.

At the beginning of the book are the easier characters to draw, they get gradually harder as the book goes on and the last few are a bit trickier than the initial ones. However, if you go through them all from the beginning, by the time you get to these you probably won't find them a problem at all! You'll be amazed at how quickly your drawing skills will develop in such a short time.

Use a pencil! You might make a few mistakes at first, but remember you can always rub them out if you're using one. You'll find the end results look a lot better also! Try and use one that doesn't have too thin a point and remember, practise makes perfect!

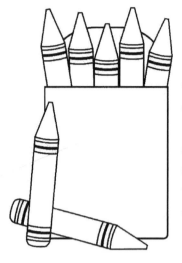

Color them in! Once you're able to draw the pictures confidently, color them in! You'll find that not only will it make them look even better but you'll enjoy it as much as drawing them in the first place. If you're going to use crayons for some of the characters, you may also need to use some coloring pencils with a thin nib as it can be quite tricky to keep crayons between the lines!

Don't give up! Remember, drawing is an art that takes practise, patience and time. Don't give up if you're finding one particular character quite difficult to draw. Leave it and move on to a slightly easier one. You will develop your skills throughout this book and you may decide to come back to certain ones at a later time. This is totally okay, you can't be a master straight away – that would be boring!

How long should each character take?

It will take as long as it takes! Don't be pressured into thinking you have to draw these characters in under a few minutes, it really doesn't matter. Initially, it will take some time. You might take half an hour on one and then decide it's rubbish and throw it away. This is fine, next time you try it won't take as long and you probably won't make the same mistake. As long as you're enjoying it then actually, the longer it takes, the better, right?

Where do I start?

From the beginning! Okay, that's obvious – but it's good advice. Start with the easy ones and work your way through them. As for each drawing, you'll end up probably adopting the same strategy for each one. That is:

- Initially do the outline of the character, it's actually the most important bit of the whole character. If you get this right, you'll find the rest of the picture is quite easy.
- Add some detail to the face and the body, it is this that actually defines the character itself and is just as important as the initial outline. It can actually be harder that the outline as it is the detail that really defines who the character is.
- The final touches. This can include some shading or ideally some coloring! Don't feel like you have to follow all the rules all the time. Use your imagination and if you want to color Pikachu bright red instead of yellow, do it! It's your drawing and you're in control, remember that!
- Most importantly, have fun!

Anyway, enough rambling on, time to make a start. Good luck!

Snorlax

Species	Sleeping	Weakness	Fighting
Type	Normal	Evolves From	Munchlax
Abilities	Immunity, Thick Fat	Weight (lbs)	1,014

Difficulty Level:

1 One of the simpler characters to draw and a great one to start with, sketch the outline...

2 ...draw the inner lines and add the claws.

3 Add in the slits for the eyes and a pair of fangs and you're done. Simple!

7

Koffing

Species	Poison Gas	Weakness	Psychic
Type	Poison	Evolves To	Weezing
Abilities	Levitate	Height (ft)	2'

Difficulty Level:

1 The Koffing is basically a circle with a few bumps around the edge. Don't worry about getting exactly the right number or getting each in the right place, it doesn't matter!

2 Add the facial features and skull and crossbones!

3 You're done apart from the clouds around it. It doesn't matter where you put them. Color the main character in purple and the clouds in a grey/green color.

Weedle

Species	Hairy Bug	Weakness	Flying, Fire, Rock, Psychic
Type	Bug, Poison	Evolves To	Kakuna
Abilities	Shield Dust	Height (ft)	1'

Difficulty Level:

1

To draw this little bug, use a series of circles, all connected. It doesn't matter if you have a few more or less than what we've got here, it'll still look good.

2 Add some more circles to Weedle's body for its legs.

3 Finally, add the detail in its eyes. When coloring, my recommendation would be to use brown for its body and purple for its nose and legs. However, if you choose to use pink for its body and silver for its nose and legs, that's ok too! This is YOUR drawing!

Oddish

Species	Weed	Weakness	Flying, Fire, Ice, Psychic
Type	Grass, Poison	Evolves To	Gloom
Abilities	Chlorophyll	Height (ft)	1' 8"

Difficulty Level:

1 This cheeky weed is quite easy to draw, start with a slightly squashed circle, add its legs before moving on to the leaves on the top.

2 Add the cheeky little face!

3 Add a little line in its mouth, a couple of marks on its feet and don't forget the leaf lines – doesn't it look great?

Zubat

Species	Bat	Weakness	Psychic, Rock, Ice, Electric
Type	Poison, Flying	Evolves To	Golbat
Abilities	Inner Focus	Height (ft)	2' 7"

Difficulty Level:

1 If you've been working through all these pictures in order, this will be no problem for you. This bat is going to look scary, that's your goal!

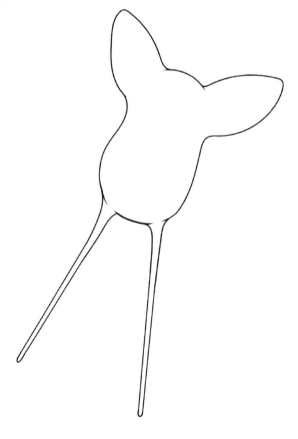

2 The key here is to get Zubat's mouth right. This is the scariest part and needs to be quite large with fangs visible!

3 Complete the wings and add some shading to its mouth to make it look really big! Concentrate when coloring its legs, they're very thin!

Horsea

Species	Dragon	Weakness	Grass, Electric
Type	Water	Evolves To	Seadra
Abilities	Sniper, Swift Swim	Height (ft)	1' 4"

Difficulty Level:

1 One of my favorites to draw, once you do it a couple of times you'll find this really easy. Take your time with the curl on its tail.

2 Add the eye detail and snout.

3 Finally, add the lines on its chest, add the eyeball and start to color in. Enjoy!

Jigglypuff

Species	Balloon	Weakness	Steel, Poison
Type	Normal, Fairy	Evolves To	Wigglytuff
Abilities	Competitive, Cute Charm	Evolves From	Igglybuff

Difficulty Level:

1 Okay, I admit it – I love this character's name! You can start with a rough circle, add its feet, arms and ears.

2 Now, add the face and the curl that extends down over its forehead.

3 Finally, add the detail in its face and ears before you start to color. This is easy, just use pink! For its eyes it's up to you! I think blue looks great but try brown and green also.

Chikorita

Species	Leaf	Weakness	Flying, Bug, Ice, Fire, Poison
Type	Grass	Evolves To	Bayleef
Abilities	Overgrow	First appearance	Pokémon Red and Blue

Difficulty Level:

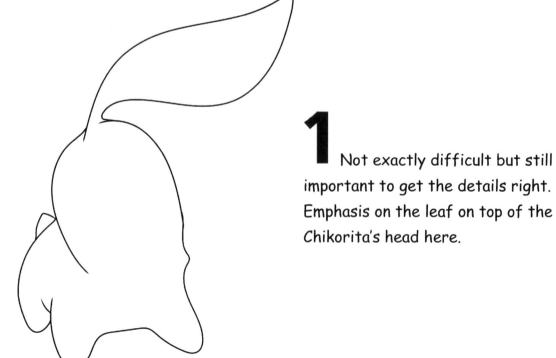

1 Not exactly difficult but still important to get the details right. Emphasis on the leaf on top of the Chikorita's head here.

2 When adding the eyes, just focus on the left side – this will give a nice effect of the character looking to one side.

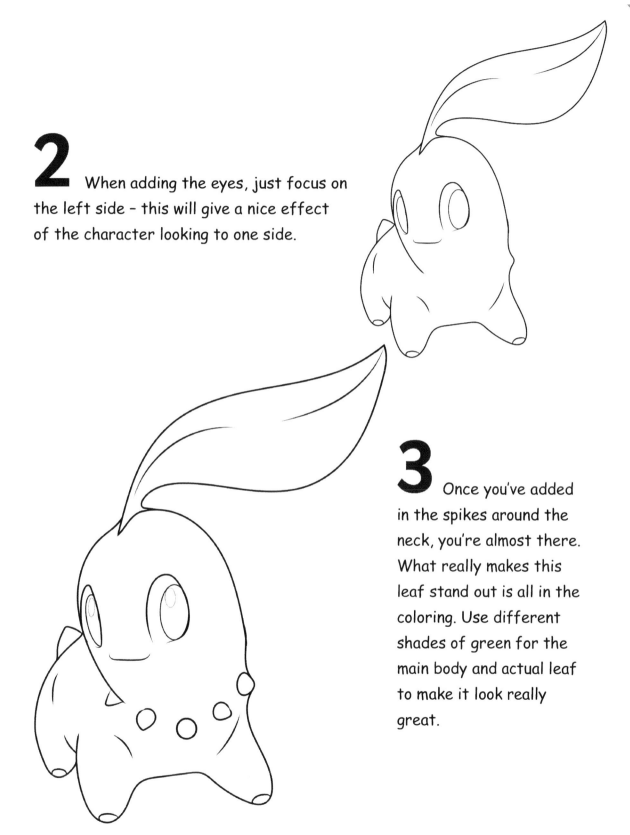

3 Once you've added in the spikes around the neck, you're almost there. What really makes this leaf stand out is all in the coloring. Use different shades of green for the main body and actual leaf to make it look really great.

Pichu

Species	Tiny Mouse	Weakness	Ground
Type	Electric	Evolves To	Pikachu
Abilities	Static	Height (ft)	1'

Difficulty Level:

1 Draw the outline as per the image on the right. You'll find Pichu is actually one of the simplest characters to draw!

22

2 Next, complete the eyes, mouth and blushing cheeks.

3 Add a little bit of shading, and remembering to color in Pichu's blushing cheeks, you're done!

Voltrob

Species	Ball	Weakness	Ground
Type	Electric	Evolves To	Electrode
Abilities	Soundproof, Static	First appearance	Pokémon Red and Blue

Difficulty Level:

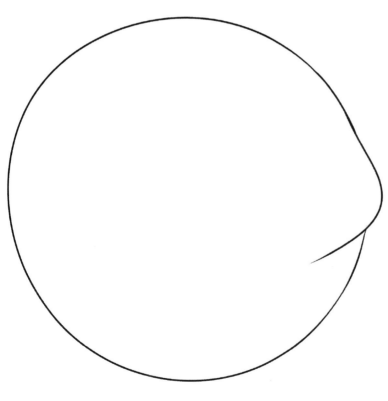

1 Initially you might think this one will only take a few seconds, but concentration will be needed later! Okay, it might start simple enough but it does get a little more challenging...

2 Make sure you get the angles of his eyebrows right, they're key to everything else!

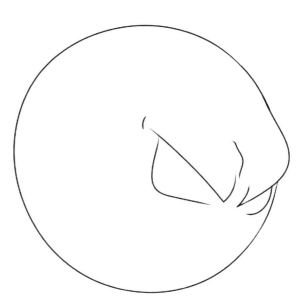

3 Just add his evil eyes and horizontal line around the ball and you're done. When coloring, don't forget the top half is a different color to the bottom half!

25

Poliwag

Species	Tadpole	Weakness	Electric, Grass
Type	Water	Evolves To	Poliwhirl
Abilities	Water Absorb, Damp	Height (ft)	2'

Difficulty Level:

1 Poliwag is a tadpole and the initial shape isn't quite a circle so be careful, more of a flattened egg!

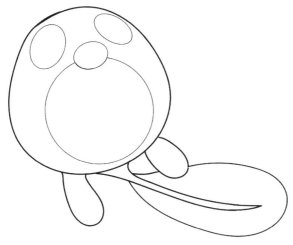

2 Add the features of the face, it's quite hard to get the right proportions here but the key is to get the nose quite a bit higher than central.

3 Now comes the really tricky bit! Poliwag has a spiral shaped mouth. The best way to approach this is to start at the centre and work your way out.

Caterpie

Species	Worm	Weakness	Flying, Fire, Rock
Type	Bug	Evolves To	Metapod
Abilities	Shield Dust	Height (ft)	1'

Difficulty Level:

1 This bug is similar to Weedle, but there are differences which you'll see when you're finished!

2 Add the antennae and some more detail around its body.

3 Add the detail in Caterpie's eyes and you're just about there. When coloring use a yellow for its belly and a green for the rest. Use an orange or red for its antennae. Complete!

Happiny

Species	Playhouse	Weakness	Fighting
Type	Normal	Evolves To	Chansey
Abilities	Serene Grace, Natural Cure	Height (ft)	2'

Difficulty Level:

1 Although quite a small character, not an easy one to draw. To begin with get the body and head shapes right and then the feet and hair...just keep it simple.

2 You may need to spend a little bit of time getting the mouth right on Happiny, it's what your eyes are drawn to first. Then add the other two bumps on its forehead, eye outlines and hands.

3 Finally shade the eyes, leaving white ovals for pupils, and add one more curve around its middle. To colour in, you should use pale pink, primarily and some dark pink for its cheeks, if you decide to shade them in.

Bellsprout

Species	Flower	Weakness	Flying, Ice, Fire, Psychic
Type	Poison, Grass	Evolves To	Weepinbell
Abilities	Chlorophyll	First appearance	Pokémon Red and Blue

Difficulty Level:

1 Time for a bit of a change, Bellsprout can be a little trickier than you first think. Its 'legs' are quite thin and if you're thinking of coloring it in you'll need to be very careful.

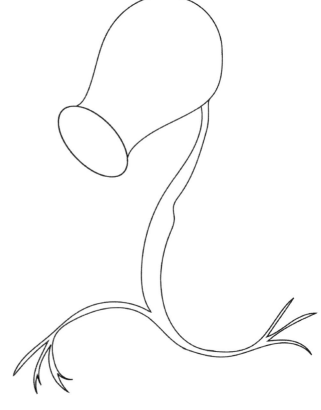

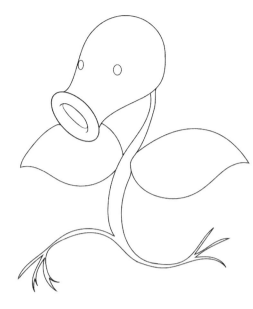

2 Pop a couple of eyes on the flower and add a squashed circle to its mouth to give a 3-d effect.

3 Add some lines to the stalk and the leaves and shade in where required, finished!

Pikachu

Species	Mouse	Weakness	Ground
Type	Electric	Evolves From	Pichu
Abilities	Static	Evolves To	Raichu

Difficulty Level:

1

As always, start with the outer border first. Get this done and you're 90% there. With Pikachu it's important to remember his zig-zag tail!

2 With the hard work now done, draw little circles for the eyes and complete the face and ears.

3 All that remains is the shading-in of Pikachu's eyes, ears and part of his tail. Just leave a little circle in each of his eyes to give him that final touch. Don't forget to color him in!

Magikarp

Species	Fish	Weakness	Electric, Grass
Type	Water	Evolves To	Gyarados
Abilities	Swift Swim	First appearance	Pokémon Red and Blue

Difficulty Level:

1 Slightly more challenging, the Magikarp. The basic outline is shown here and can be quite tricky. Don't worry if you don't get it right the first time!

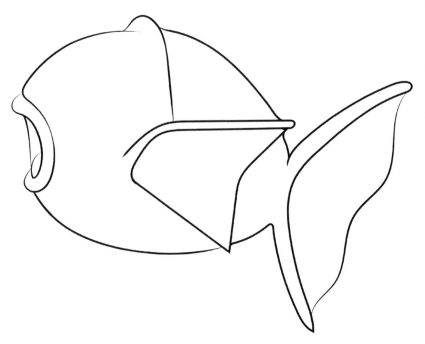

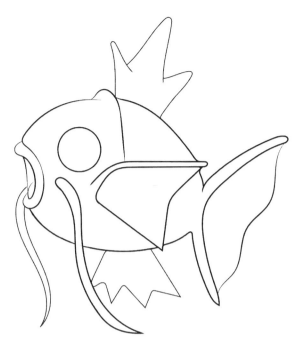

2 Adding in quite a lot more detail now, lots of curvy lines make the Magikarp a challenge.

3 Not much left to do at this point, you may want to color in the top and bottom fins a different color to its tail.

Lickitung

Species	Licking	Weakness	Fighting
Type	Normal	Evolves To	Lickilicky
Abilities	Oblivious, Own Tempo	Height (ft)	3' 11"

Difficulty Level:

1 Although not exactly easy, Lickitung has quite a simple outline but don't forget his massive tongue!

2 Add his face and a line down the middle of his tongue, see what a difference this makes.

3 Add the stripes to his tummy and knees then shade in his nostrils and eyes, you're done – lick!

Clefairy

Species	Fairy	Weakness	Steel, Poison
Type	Fairy	Evolves To	Cleffa
Abilities	Magic Guard, Cute Charm	Evolves from	Clefable

Difficulty Level:

1 Certainly not the easiest but also not the hardest. Take care when drawing the spiral as you want the end of it to stop in the middle of its forehead.

2 Add the face, the key feature with this one is the happy mouth!

3 Finally, add some shading to add emphasis to its ears and eyes, put your pencil down and have a break, you're doing great!

Slowpoke

Species	Dopey	Weakness	Ghost, Dark, Electric, Bug, Grass
Type	Psychic, Water	Evolves To	Slowbro, Slowking
Abilities	Oblivious, Own Tempo	First appearance	Pokémon Red and Blue

Difficulty Level:

1 Slowpoke is initially a little tricky. Concentrate on getting the body and head right, before adding the tail, ears, and legs.

2 Now add the eyes, nostrils, mouth details and teeth.

3 Finally, a couple of dots create the pupils in its eyes, one last curve in its mouth gives him a tongue and claws complete his feet.

Sandshrew

Species	Mouse	Weakness	Ice, Grass, Water
Type	Ground	Evolves To	Sandslash
Abilities	Sand Veil	Height (ft)	2'

Difficulty Level:

1 Pay attention to the chin of the Sandshrew, it needs to be quite pointy! One of the trickier outlines to get right first time but practice makes perfect!

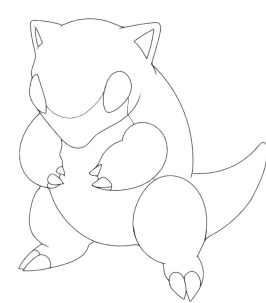

2 Add the claws and face features, not forgetting the inside of his ears.

3 The Sandshrew has quite a lot of scales, don't worry about getting them exactly like this, close enough will do. Shade in the eyes and leave little glints of light.

Muk

Species	Sludge	Weakness	Ground, Psychic
Type	Poison	Evolves To	Grimer
Abilities	Stench, Sticky Hold	Height (ft)	3' 11"

Difficulty Level:

★★★★☆

1 An unusual looking monster, don't worry about getting the wobbly lines exactly right.

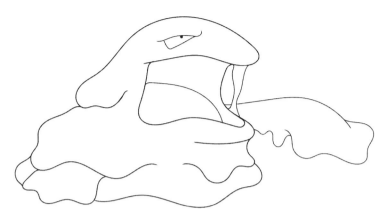

2

The important but here
are the Muk's slimy face
and evil looking eye!

3

Add a few wavy lines and when coloring use a slightly darker shade for these.

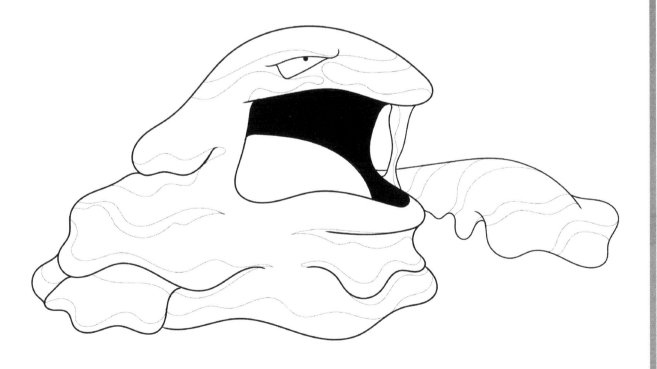

Bulbasaur

Species	Seed	Weakness	Psychic, Ice, Fire, Flying
Type	Grass, Poison	Evolves To	Ivysaur
Abilities	Overgrow	First appearance	Pokémon Red and Blue

Difficulty Level:

1 A relatively simple outline but can get a little tricky later when adding the detail. If you can't quite get the edges of its claws, don't worry – you can put those in later.

2 Now you add its mouth and eyes, make them really big.

3 Add some shapes to its body and a bit of detail to the eyes and you're finished. For the body just use different shades of green, and color its eyes in a pinky-red color.

Charmander

Species	Lizard	Weakness	Rock, Ground, Water
Type	Fire	Evolves To	Charmeleon
Abilities	Blaze	First appearance	Pokémon Red and Blue

Difficulty Level:

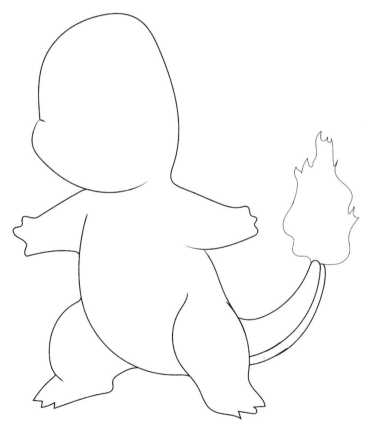

1 Certainly not one of the easiest to draw but also not one of the most difficult. Get the outer shape done and remember the end of its tail is on fire, draw that how you like!

2 As usual, now add some detail into its face and add the claws.

3 Add in the final detail to his face and start coloring. This one is fun as you can do its tail any way you like...as long as it looks like it's on fire! Use yellow, orange and red for this.

Squirtle

Species	Tiny Turtle	Weakness	Grass, Electric
Type	Water	Evolves To	Wartortle
Abilities	Torrent	First appearance	Pokémon Red and Blue

Difficulty Level:

1 Start with two circles for this Turtle's body and head. Add the legs, arms and the tail, not forgetting the little curl at the end!

2 As usual at this stage, add the detail into Squirtle's face and a couple of lines to distinguish the shell on its back.

3 Add the detail in the face and the lines on Squirtle's belly and you're done!

Eevee

Species	Evolution	Weakness	Fighting
Type	Normal	Evolves To	Several
Abilities	Adaptability, Run Away	First appearance	Pokémon Red and Blue

Difficulty Level:

1 Not as hard as you might initially think but still a bit tricky. Make sure you get its long ears and tail right before working on the fantastic fur that this cute character has.

2 Add Eevee's face and a little more detail inside its ears.

3 Spend a little more time detailing the eyes and ears and you're done. When coloring, use browns for the main body and a slightly lighter brown for its fur.

Vulpix

Species	Fox	Weakness	Rock, Water, Ground
Type	Fire	Evolves To	Ninetales
Abilities	Flash Fire	Height (ft)	2'

Difficulty Level:

1 This cute little fox is actually one of the most difficult characters to draw. The little paws may take some practice but don't give up. Once you've cracked this one you'll be able to draw anything!

2 The Vulpix has a little cute nose that needs to be captured just right, make sure it's small and in the right place.

3 All the hard work has finally paid off now and with the little details to its face complete you can sit back and admire your work!

Psyduck

Species	Duck	Weakness	Grass, Electric
Type	Water	Evolves To	Golduck
Abilities	Cloud Nine, Damp	First appearance	Pokémon Red and Blue

Difficulty Level:

1 This is quite a tricky character to draw, harder than it looks initially. Concentrate on getting the body and head right, then work on the other bits before moving on.

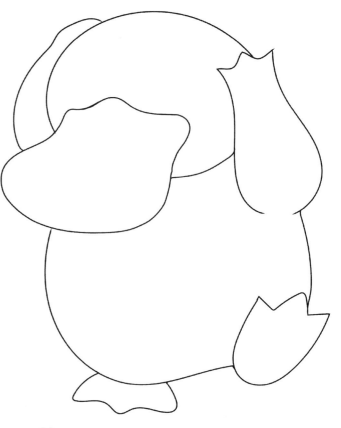

2 Add its eyes and a couple of lines to his beak before moving on.

3 Not much more too add, the three small lines sticking out of the top of its head are what identifies this duck, don't forget them!

Geodude

Species	Rock	Weakness	Ground, Ice, Water, Grass, Steel, Fighting
Type	Ground, Rock	Evolves To	Graveler
Abilities	Sturdy, Rock Head	Weight (lbs)	44

Difficulty Level:

1

The Geodude is one of the trickier characters to draw, primarily because it is a rock and there are a lot of bumps in it. Don't worry about getting the below exactly right, just focus on it looking 'rocky'.

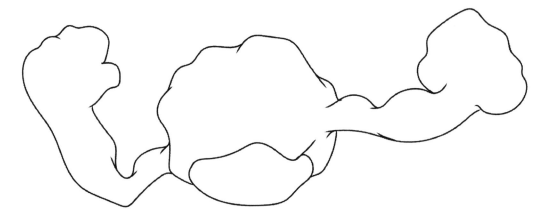

2

Add some more detail to the rock, a few lines here and there add some perspective.

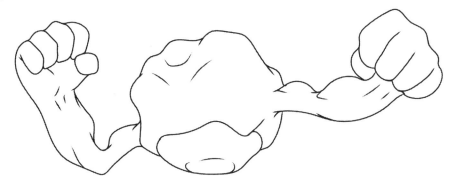

3

The finishing touches really make this look like Geodude. Add the eyes, making sure the eyebrows both point inwards, this will give it a very aggressive look!

Meowth

Species	Scratch Cat	Weakness	Fighting
Type	Normal	Evolves To	Persian
Abilities	Pickup / Technician	First Appearance	Pokémon Red and Blue

Difficulty Level:

1 Not your ordinary cat, what makes Meowth stand-out is the two whiskers that appear to be sticking straight-up from his head, don't forget these! What might appear quite complex at first, when broken down actually isn't, and once you get the hang of it you'll be able to do these outlines in a matter of seconds!

2 For the next step, complete Meowth's mouth and eyes.

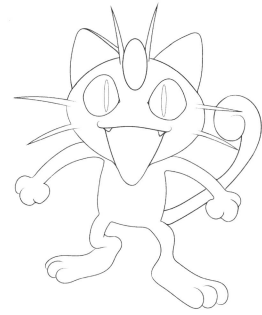

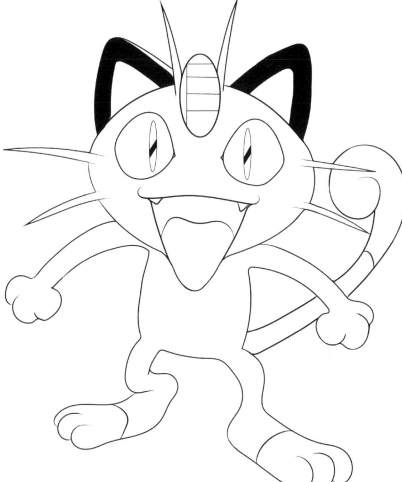

3 Finally, a bit of shading for his ears (maybe a darker color), add some detail to his tongue and eyes and you're there!

Raichu

Species	Mouse	Weakness	Ground
Type	Electric	Evolves To	Pikachu
Abilities	Static	Height	2'7"

Difficulty Level:

1 The body is one of the trickier to draw and just check out those ears! If they prove too difficult, don't worry, you can always leave the squiggle out. Don't be put off by the five-star difficulty rating, you can do this!

2 As you can see, Raichu certainly isn't the easiest of characters to draw. Just ensure you get the tail and face correct and it'll certainly be recognizable!

3 Only a few more details now around his face, arms and feet.

Finally...

Thank you so much for buying (and getting to the end) of my book! I hope you've had a great time learning how to draw these Pokémon Go characters. I've been a fan of this game since it came out and have spent more time than you can imagine getting these images just right for the beginner (and more advanced) to be able to copy and draw them for themselves. Some people find drawing easier than others, don't worry if it's taking you a bit longer than you'd hoped. If you practise with your favorite characters then I can promise you that you will eventually be able to draw them, not only very well but from memory!

If you liked this book, perhaps you'll like 'Love to Draw...MORE Pokémon Go' – 30 more characters for you to learn how to draw, check it out on Amazon now!

If you'd like to get in touch with me personally, my email address is at the bottom of this page.

Printed in Poland
by Amazon Fulfillment
Poland Sp. z o.o., Wrocław